Seahorse
Stars

Seahorse Stars

The Rainbow Queen

Zuzu Singer

Illustrated by Helen Turner

USBORNE

Meet the Pearlies

Shy but sweet CORA is a pretty pink seahorse with pale pink stripes.

Fun and friendly CAMMIE is a vivid pink seahorse who dreams of becoming a Seahorse Star.

Bossyboots CORINETTA is a golden seahorse with a snooty upturned nose.

Cammie's best friend JESS is a born storyteller. She is a bright bluey-green.

# of Rainbow Reef

Pale-green
MISS SWISH
is firm but fair
as the elegant
leader of
the Pearlies.

Brainbox BREE
knows all the answers!
She is purple with lovely
lavender fins.

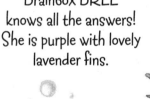

Fast and fearless
FIZZ has bold red and
yellow stripes and is
ready for anything!

Rainbow Reef

Coral Tower

Seahorse City

Eelgrass forest

Palace

Sandy Cove

Pearlie Pavilion

Cammie's House

Pink Sand Plains

Coral Caves

Seahorse Stars is dedicated to every child who
loves to read...including you!

First published in the UK in 2011 by Usborne Publishing Ltd., Usborne
House, 83-85 Saffron Hill, London EC1N 8RT, England.
www.usborne.com

Text copyright © Lee Weatherly, 2011

Illustration copyright © Usborne Publishing Ltd., 2011

A CIP catalogue record for this book is available from the British Library.

JFMAMJJA OND/11 02344/1

ISBN 9781409520313 Printed in Reading, Berkshire, UK.

Chapter One

Cammie Sunbeam felt giddy with excitement as she and her best friend Jess swam side by side through Rainbow Reef. "I can't believe it!" she exclaimed, darting past a piece of yellow coral. "Today's the day we're finally going to find out about our sixth pearl."

Jess nodded eagerly. She was a pretty

blue-green seahorse, while Cammie was a bright, cheerful pink. "And then after that, we'll finally be…"

"*Seahorse Stars!*" cried both girls, twirling on their tails.

The Seahorse Stars was the waviest club in Rainbow Reef. They got to go on exciting trips, and do projects that helped the Reef and its creatures. Cammie could hardly wait to be one!

And for the first time, it seemed like she was almost there. Cammie gazed proudly up at her crown, where five gleaming pearls sat. She and Jess were both Pearlies, and had earned their pearls for learning different skills that Seahorse Stars had to know. As soon as they earned their sixth, they'd finally be Seahorse Stars.

Cammie smiled as the pink coral walls of the Pearlie Pavilion came into view. Until then, though, being a Pearlie was the next best thing. And their Pearlie meeting today should be brilliant. Finally, they'd find out what they needed to do for their sixth pearl!

Then Cammie bit her lip worriedly. What if she wasn't able to get her final pearl? Some of them had been really difficult to earn. It would be awful to come so far and then not become a Seahorse Star after all!

"What's wrong?" asked Jess as they swam around a clump of eelgrass.

Cammie tried to smile. "Oh, nothing," she said. "I was just—" She broke off as a shadow crossed the white sand below. Glancing up, she thought she saw a strange shape drifting across the water's surface...and then it vanished from view.

Jess turned on her tail, gazing off in the same direction. "What are you looking at?"

Cammie blinked. What *had* she been
looking at? Whatever it was, it was gone now.
"Um — I'm not sure," she said. "I thought I saw
something, but..." She shrugged. "Never mind.
I guess I was wrong."

The two friends swam through the arched
doorway of the Pearlie Pavilion together.

Dozens of other young seahorses were just arriving, too. They were every colour of the rainbow, all of them with five pearls shining on their crowns.

Cammie looked around her happily. No matter how many times she entered the Pearlie Pavilion, she never got tired of it. Its curved walls were such a pretty pink, and it had an open ceiling that showed the sun sparkling on the water.

"Cammie! Jess!" called a voice from behind them. Turning, Cammie saw Fizz, one of the other seahorses in their group. Fizz had red and yellow stripes, and was very sporty. A clever purple seahorse called Bree was with her. As usual, Bree had a shell-book under her fin that she'd been reading.

"What do you two think our last pearl
will be for?" asked Fizz eagerly, catching them
up. The tasks that Pearlies needed to do to
become Seahorse Stars were always kept a
secret — which made being a Pearlie even
more exciting!

"We don't know," said Cammie. "But we can hardly wait to find out."

"Me too," said Bree, adjusting her glasses. "I can't believe that we're nearly Seahorse Stars!"

The four seahorses swam together to the area where their group, the Dancing Waves, met. The other two girls, Cora and Corinetta, were already there, sitting perched on seashell chairs. Cora, a nervous, pale-pink seahorse, looked relieved to see them arrive. Cammie wasn't surprised. Corinetta was very snooty at times, and not the easiest seahorse to get along with!

"Oh, hello," drawled Corinetta when she saw them. She was a golden colour, and had an unusually tall crown of which she was very proud. "We were just talking about our sixth pearl."

"I know! None of us can imagine what it's going to be for," said Jess as they all took a seat.

Corinetta looked smug. "Really? Well, *I* know."

Cora sighed. "She *says* she knows. But she won't tell me what it is!"

"How could you know?" demanded Fizz of Corinetta.

She gave a sneering smile. "I just do, that's all. And I've already started working on my project, too. I started days ago!"

Bree's jaw dropped. "But — that's not fair! That means that you got a head start, and the rest of us didn't."

"What a shame," yawned Corinetta. "Never mind. Maybe you'll all still get your sixth pearls anyway."

Cammie scowled at her. Though Corinetta could be all right at times, usually she wasn't! Cammie thought that the Pearlies would be much more fun if she wasn't in their group.

"Hello, girls!" said a cheerful voice. Miss Swish, the leader of the Dancing Waves, came swimming up. She was a tall, pale-green seahorse with wise eyes and a friendly expression.

"Hi, Miss Swish," said the girls. Cammie smiled to see her. Miss Swish could be very firm, but she was always fair — and she knew everything there was to know about becoming a Seahorse Star!

Miss Swish shook her head as she gazed at them. "I can hardly believe that we're on the sixth pearl already! You've all done such a good job so far. Are you ready to hear about your final pearl?"

Cammie nodded with the others. Excitement tingled through her. Finally — they were about to hear what their last pearl would be! Out of the corner of her eye, she saw Corinetta smirk.

Miss Swish went to the front of their area, where a piece of slate rested on a coral stand. Picking up a bit of chalk, she wrote the words, FRIEND TO THE REEF in swirling letters.

"Your sixth pearl is for doing something to help Rainbow Reef," she explained. "That might mean doing something to help the Reef itself, such as planting a seaweed garden, or cleaning a piece of coral. Or, you might do something to help the community that lives here. For instance, you could paint a mural for a building, or do volunteer work to help others."

Cammie listened eagerly. Their sixth pearl sounded amazing! She loved Rainbow Reef, and could hardly wait to do something to help it. But what?

Corinetta's eyes had grown wide. "But — I thought the sixth pearl was being a friend to *ourselves*," she burst out. "I thought I was supposed to be doing something to help ME!

So I've been making myself a new mirror, with pretty shells all around it, and—" She broke off with a scowl as everyone started laughing.

Miss Swish looked amused too. "Ah, Corinetta...I did think that perhaps you overheard me last week, when I was talking to one of the other group leaders about the sixth pearl. I'm sorry that you got it wrong." Her eyes were twinkling.

"But at least she has a new mirror, to admire her crown in!" whispered Jess in Cammie's ear. Cammie stifled a giggle. The expression on Corinetta's face was a picture!

"Remember the Pearlie Rule, Corinetta," went on Miss Swish. "To think of others before ourselves, and to do a good turn every

day. That's what this pearl is all about —
helping others, not ourselves!"

Corinetta nodded sullenly. "Yes, Miss
Swish," she muttered.

"Now then," said Miss Swish, putting the
chalk down. "Let's all get in a circle and talk
about what you'd like to do!"

Chapter Two

The Dancing Waves all pulled their seashell chairs into a circle, so that they were facing each other. "Now, does anyone know already what they'd like to do?" asked Miss Swish.

Cammie wasn't surprised when Bree's fin shot up. The clever purple seahorse was always the first with an answer. However, she was so nice that everyone liked her anyway!

"Yes, Bree?" said Miss Swish.

"I'm going to do volunteer work for the Rainbow Reef Library!" exclaimed Bree, her eyes shining behind her glasses.

"An excellent idea," said Miss Swish warmly. "I know that Miss Sand could use some extra help. Who else knows what they're doing? Yes, Fizz?"

"I'm going to set up a court for playing coral ball," said Fizz, bouncing on her striped tail. "There's a place near my house that would be perfect! I bet all the young seahorses would have a lot of fun playing it."

"Very good!" praised Miss Swish. "We could use more play areas in Rainbow Reef. That's something that will really aid the community."

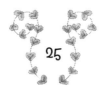

Cammie bit her lip as she listened. Both Bree's and Fizz's ideas sounded fantastic! She wanted to do something just as useful as they were…only she didn't have a clue what.

"I'm going to plant a seaweed garden," said Cora when it was her turn. "My father knows all about the different types of seaweed you can use for healing. I'm going to plant lots of

them, so that any seahorse who needs a certain
kind can have some!"

Jess's idea was great, too — she was going to
clean a smudged section of coral near her house.
And even Corinetta had a good idea, now that
she'd got over her shock about the pearl. She
planned to read stories to the young seahorses
at the school where her mother taught.

"I think I'll do that *really* well," she said grandly. "I'm very dramatic, you know! Remember how well I acted my part during our dance, when we earned our last pearl?"

Miss Swish seemed to be holding back a smile. "Good idea, Corinetta. Cammie? What about you?"

Cammie's mind was racing. All the best ideas seemed to be taken already. She couldn't think of a single thing that she wanted to do! "Um…" she said, tapping the tip of her tail against her chair.

"It's fine if you haven't decided yet," said Miss Swish kindly.

"You could help me clean the coral," offered Jess. "Would that be okay, Miss Swish?"

Their leader nodded. "Yes, you can work in

pairs if you like. Would you like to do that, Cammie?"

Cammie hesitated. Though it would be lots of fun to work with Jess, she knew that she'd rather have a project of her own — something special that she'd thought of herself. "Maybe," she said finally.

Miss Swish smiled. "Well, you don't have to decide just yet. Why don't you go for a long swim later, and see if any ideas come to you? Then you can tell me at the next meeting what you've decided."

Cammie nodded, feeling a bit glum. Everyone else had known right away what they wanted to do, and their ideas were all so good! She wished that she could help her mum, who was one of the guards who protected Rainbow

Reef, but knew she wouldn't be allowed to do that until she was older.

When Pearlies was over with, Cammie and Jess swam home together. Cammie sighed as she looked around her. Rainbow Reef was so beautiful, with all its bright colours — pink and yellow coral, and purple stones, and white sand. *Why* couldn't she think of something to do to help it?

"Don't worry, you'll figure out what you want to do soon," said Jess, squeezing Cammie's tail. "And if you don't, then you can just help me! That wouldn't be so terrible, would it?" She grinned.

Cammie laughed. "No, I guess it wouldn't be *too* bad." She smiled at Jess, feeling a bit better. Even so, she was determined to find her own idea. She was going to make sure that her sixth pearl was for something really special!

But though Cammie spent the next few days thinking hard, no ideas came to mind. Finally, remembering Miss Swish's suggestion, she decided to go for a long swim. Maybe that would help her decide what to do.

"Cammie, where are you going?" asked Tigg, her little sister, as Cammie started out the door.

"Just for a swim," said Cammie. "I'm trying to decide how I can help the Reef, so that I can earn my sixth pearl." Then she almost groaned aloud. *Why* had she said that? Tigg could hardly wait to be a Pearlie herself. She was sure to want to come along now!

Sure enough, Tigg's eyes grew wide. "Ooh, can I help?" she cried, bobbing up and down in the water. "Please, Cammie? Please please please?"

"Yes, all right," sighed Cammie. "You can come with me, but you have to be *very* quiet, and let me think."

Cammie's little brother Stripe came drifting out of the lounge, looking bored. He and Tigg were twins, and both had vivid orange and black stripes. "Think about what?" he asked.

"About what she's going to do for her sixth pearl!" burst out Tigg. "We're going on a long swim to decide. And *I'm* going to help!"

Stripe's face lit up. "Can I come, too?" he asked eagerly. "I'm good at thinking of ideas!"

Cammie winced. Oh, great, just what she needed — her little brother *and* her little sister! Still, maybe the two of them would keep each other company, and leave her alone. "Okay," she said grumpily. "But you have to keep *quiet,* and let me think."

They started off, gliding down the sandy lane outside the Sunbeams' house. "How about this, Cammie?" said Tigg, dashing ahead to point at a large rock.

Cammie blinked. "What about it?"

Tigg's face screwed up in thought. "Um, I don't know. You could paint it, maybe, or... or move it, or..."

"No, thanks," said Cammie with a sigh. "That's not what I'm looking for, Tigg."

"How about this, then?" said Stripe, grabbing at a drifting piece of seaweed. "You could...um...make clothes for the crabs out of it!" He and Tigg burst into giggles.

"Yeah!" said Tigg. She draped the seaweed around her and pretended to be a crab, waggling her fins like claws. "They'd look *soo* stylish!"

Cammie rolled her eyes. She'd never get any thinking done at this rate! "Okay, it's time for you both to go home now," she said.

Tigg's face fell. "But you said I could help!"

"You've helped already," said Cammie quickly. "You really have, Tigg! But now I just need some time on my own, all right?"

"Well...all right," said Tigg reluctantly.

Stripe tugged at her fin. "Come on — let's go and find a crab to give the seaweed to!"

Cammie shook her head with a smile as the two of them jetted off, giggling. Finally! She had some time on her own.

She swam and swam, gazing at the reef around her. *I could plant a seaweed garden,* she thought, gazing at a clump of yellow seaweed. But no, Cora was already doing that.

Then a silver fish flashed past, with lots of baby fishes darting along behind. *Or I could do something to help the Rainbow Reef children,* Cammie mused. But Fizz and Corinetta were already doing projects that

helped the youngsters of Rainbow Reef.
Cammie wanted to do something different,
that was hers alone.

After a while, she came to a part of the
Reef that she wasn't familiar with. She looked
around her curiously, taking in the bright green
coral and white sand. Maybe there was
something around here that would give her
an idea.

Then she jumped as a cross voice
demanded, "What are you doing here? Go
away, you're not wanted!"

Chapter Three

Whirling around, Cammie saw a hermit crab on the sand. He was peering suspiciously up at her, his eyes waving about on their stalks. "I – I'm sorry," she stammered. "I didn't know I wasn't supposed to be here."

. The crab *harrumphed*. "Well…I suppose it's all right," he said grumpily. "So long as you don't clutter anything up."

Looking around, Cammie saw that she was in front of a very tidy cave. Its coral walls were polished, and the white sand in front of it had been swept clean. A shiny nameplate over the doorway read *Archibald Crab*.

"That's me," said the crab, pointing to the sign with his claw. He puffed out his chest proudly.

"Archibald Crab! I've got the nicest cave of any crab in Rainbow Reef. You can call me Archie," he added importantly.

Cammie held back a giggle. He sounded as if he were doing her a favour! "I'm Cammie," she said. "Your cave is certainly very tidy."

"Yes, I know," said Archie. "And I plan on keeping it that way!" Just then a bit of eelgrass went drifting past, and landed on the sand at Archie's feet. The hermit crab's eyes seemed to bulge. Snatching up the eelgrass, he scuttled away with it to the side of his cave. Then he returned with a broom, carefully sweeping the spot where the grass had fallen.

"I like things to be *just so*," he explained, putting the broom away. "I can't abide clutter, not one bit!"

Cammie nodded. "I can see that," she said gravely. She was very glad that Jess wasn't there. Archie was so fussy and particular that she knew she and her best friend wouldn't have been able to keep from bursting into laughter.

Even so, Cammie couldn't help liking the crab. Suddenly an idea popped into her head. Maybe Archie could help her decide what she should do! Quickly, Cammie told the crab how she needed to do something to help the Reef in order to earn her sixth pearl.

"Do you have any ideas?" she asked.

"Of course!" said Archie, clicking his claws.

Excitement rushed through Cammie. "You do?" she squealed.

"Yes, you could help me keep my house tidy," said Archie. "That's a very important job, young seahorse! And it *always* needs doing."

Cammie let out a disappointed breath. She

should have known! "Um...no thanks, I think I'll find something else," she said. "In fact, I suppose I'd better be going now."

Archie had just spotted a speck of sea-dust on his cave, and was polishing it vigorously with his claw. "It was nice meeting you," he said over his shell. "Come back soon — if you promise not to be untidy!"

Cammie swam on, soon leaving Archie and his cave behind. She sighed. Was she *ever* going to figure out what to do for her project? Then she saw something, and her eyes widened. What was *that*? It was like a — a huge shadow, draped over the coral.

Drawing closer, she saw that what she had thought was a shadow was actually a massive net, snagged on the coral. Cammie stared at it in horror. She could see broken pieces of coral caught in its weave. Even as she watched, the net moved with the current, and another piece of coral snapped away.

Cammie went cold as she remembered the strange object that she'd seen on her way to Pearlies the other day. Suddenly she was sure that this had been it. The net must have drifted away from a boat — and now it was damaging the delicate coral. It had to be taken away before it could hurt anything else!

Her heart thudding, Cammie dashed off as fast as she could. *Mum!* she thought as she sped frantically through the water. *I've got to tell Mum!* Her mother was one of the Rainbow Reef guards, and one of the fastest seahorses in the Reef. If anyone would know what to do, she would.

Cammie darted through a hole in a piece of coral, and then whizzed around a rock. "Watch where you're going!" called an eel. Finally Cammie arrived at the guards' tower.

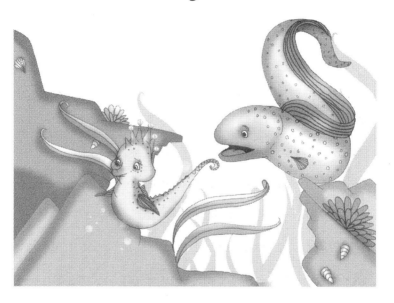

"Mum!" she called, swimming up to the tower's entrance. She was panting so hard she could barely speak. "Mum, I — I need to talk to you!"

"Cammie!" Her mother appeared, looking startled. She was the same bright, vivid pink as Cammie. "What are you doing here? Is everything all right?"

Cammie felt close to tears. "No, I've — I've seen something terrible!" she burst out. "Oh, Mum, I need your help!"

Quickly, her mother came outside and patted Cammie's fin. "Calm down, sweetie — take deep breaths! Now, tell me what's wrong."

Somehow, Cammie gasped out the whole awful story. Her mother's face became grave as she heard about the net and the broken coral. "This is serious," she said. "You were right to come to me immediately, Cammie. We'll need to tell the Rainbow Queen."

Cammie gasped. Queen Hortense was very old and grand, and was the most respected seahorse in Rainbow Reef. Cammie had only ever seen her from a distance. "The — the *Queen*?" she squeaked.

Her mother nodded. "She needs to know about this. Just tell her exactly what you've told me, Cammie. It's very important."

"All right," said Cammie in a daze. Hardly able to believe this was happening, she swam along with her mother to the royal palace. Its purple coral towers rose high in the water, and a pair of seahorse guards stood at the doorway. They looked very important, with shiny mother-of-pearl buttons on their crowns, and sashes made of eelgrass over their chests.

Cammie's mother explained to the guards who they were. "We need to see the Queen at once," she told them. "My daughter's spotted a ghost net."

One of the guards stared down his snout at Cammie. "You have?"

Cammie nodded, realizing that "ghost net" must be what you called a net that was loose and drifting. "Yes, and it's *horrible*," she said, her voice shaking. "It's hurting the coral — we have to tell the Queen!"

As the guard quickly swam off, Cammie's mother sighed. "I just hope that Queen Hortense will let us do something about it," she murmured.

Cammie stared at her mother in confusion. "But — why wouldn't she?"

Before Cammie's mother could answer, the guard had returned. He lifted his nose in the air. "The Rainbow Queen will see you now!" he announced.

Chapter Four

Cammie gaped around her as they followed
the guard through the long hallways. Just wait
until she told Jess that she'd been inside the
palace! It was even grander than she'd
imagined. There were high ceilings, and
elaborate furniture made from shells, and rich
murals on the walls.

Finally the guard stopped in front of a set of double doors. They were made from shells, too, and gleamed as brightly as if Archie the crab had been polishing them. Opening the doors, the guard swished inside. "Your Majesty! Tessa and Cammie Sunbeam to see you."

"Enter," said a deep voice. Cammie gulped. Suddenly she was very glad that her mother was there, too. She'd be tempted to turn tail and speed off otherwise!

As they entered the room, Cammie stared at the Queen in wonder. She was a rich, royal purple, and wore a beautiful cape made of woven eelgrass. On her head was a golden crown adorned with sparkling jewels. Her eyes were wise and gentle...but Cammie thought there was something sad about them, too.

"Your Majesty," said Cammie's mother, bowing low in the water. Cammie quickly copied her, almost touching her nose to the sandy floor.

Cammie's mother explained why they were there. The Queen's expression seemed to grow even sadder. "Is this true?" she asked Cammie in her low voice.

Cammie swallowed hard. "Yes, Your Majesty," she whispered.

"Don't be afraid, my dear. Just tell me everything that happened," urged the Rainbow Queen.

Somehow, Cammie told her story. The Queen shook her head gravely. "Another net," she murmured. "Oh, just as I feared!" She stared off into the water as if remembering something.

There was a silence. Cammie fidgeted, wondering when the Queen was going to speak. Finally her mother said, "Your Majesty, I suggest that we guards take care of it. We could remove it from the coral, and—"

"No!" the Queen burst out. She shuddered. "Absolutely not. No one is to even go near the ghost net."

"But — it's hurting the coral!" exclaimed

Cammie. Then she gasped and popped her fin over her mouth. Had she really just dared to talk back to the Queen?

Her mother frowned at her, but Queen Hortense only sighed heavily. "Yes, and hurting the coral is a terrible thing. But it would be even worse if other creatures were hurt, too."

"Other creatures?" repeated Cammie in confusion.

The Queen nodded. "You see, my son, the prince, was killed many years ago, trying to move a ghost net. Since then, I've decreed that no one is to go near them — no matter what!"

Cammie's fins went cold. She had only thought about the net hurting the coral. It hadn't occurred to her that other creatures might get caught up in it, too. *But...if that's true, then it's more important than ever that we move it!* she thought fretfully.

Cammie's mother sighed. "Your Majesty, I understand your feelings, but I was hoping that we still might be allowed to try. We can't just let the net stay there—"

"Yes, we can," said the Queen sharply. "No one is to touch it — that's my command! With luck, the tide will soon take it away again."

Cammie stared at her. Queen Hortense couldn't really mean to just *leave* the ghost net there! But looking at the Rainbow Queen's stern expression, she realized that that was exactly what was going to happen.

"Can — can the guards at least put up a sign, to warn everyone?" said Cammie in a whisper. Her mother shot her a grateful glance.

The Queen inclined her head. "Yes, you may do that," she said. "But that is all!"

Cammie felt stunned as she and her mother swam back to the guards' tower. She still couldn't believe that the Rainbow Queen wasn't going to do anything! "Mum, are ghost nets really dangerous?" she asked in a tiny voice.

Her mother nodded sadly. "I'm afraid so. They do a lot of damage to coral, and it takes hundreds of years for the coral to grow back again. And creatures can become trapped in ghost nets, as well." She shook her head, looking worried. "I wish we could try to move it — but Queen Hortense has given her command."

Cammie swallowed hard. She knew that you couldn't go against what the Queen said...yet it seemed to her that the Queen was wrong. Of course, it was terrible that her son had died trying to move a ghost net. But was that really a reason for no one to ever try again, when ghost nets caused so much harm?

Seeing her expression, her mother patted her fin. "Don't worry, Cammie. The other guards and I will put a sign up, so that no one will go near the net. And who knows — maybe the tide *will* carry it away soon!"

Cammie bit her lip. "But — if the tide carries it away, then it will be drifting on its own. Wouldn't that be even *more* dangerous? Creatures could get tangled up in it!"

Her mother sighed. "I know it's awful, Cammie, but there's nothing more we can do. I'll do my best to keep an eye on the net, so that it won't hurt anyone."

"But—" Cammie started.

Her mother laid a fin over her mouth. "It's a grown-up problem," she said gently. "Try not to worry about it, okay?"

Cammie stared down at the white sand floor. "Okay," she said finally.

"Good girl," said her mother warmly, squeezing her tail. "And you were right to come and tell me. Go on home, now. I'll be there soon."

Cammie swam glumly towards home, her thoughts spinning like a whirlpool. How could she not worry about the ghost net? It was probably still snagged on the coral right now, breaking pieces off it. And the thought of it coming loose and drifting was even worse. Cammie imagined swimming along and suddenly becoming trapped in a net, and shivered.

"Cammie!" called a voice.

Turning, Cammie saw Jess speeding towards her. Her friend was carrying a shell bucket and a sponge. "I've just been cleaning that piece of coral near my house," she said cheerfully, swirling to a stop in front of Cammie. "It's looking better already! Have you thought of a project to do for your sixth pearl yet?"

Cammie had forgotten all about it! "No, um...not yet," she mumbled.

Jess's expression turned to one of concern. "What's wrong? You look really upset."

Taking a deep breath, Cammie told her. Jess's eyes grew wide in horror. "But that's awful!" she burst out. "You mean that the ghost net's just going to sit there, snapping off pieces of coral every time it moves?"

Cammie nodded. "Unless…it starts to drift," she said weakly.

Jess went pale. Cammie knew that her best friend was thinking of all the creatures who might become trapped in the net if that happened. "Wow," she whispered finally. "I — I wish that we could do something. But I guess that Queen Hortense knows best. She's very wise, after all."

Cammie's heart felt heavy. "I suppose," she said finally.

The two friends made their way towards home, swimming around pieces of bright pink and yellow coral. Cammie gazed sadly around her. It was all so pretty — but not far away, the ghost net was damaging coral that was every bit as beautiful.

Cammie sighed. She wished that she could be as sure as Jess that Queen Hortense's decision had been the right one...but she wasn't.

Chapter Five

Cammie couldn't put the ghost net out of her mind. She still felt worried that night, as she ate dinner with her family.

"Stripe, Tigg, eat your stew and stop messing about," ordered their father. He was a blue seahorse with a cheerful twinkle in his eye. Though he didn't look very cheerful at the

moment, as he dealt with Cammie's little brother and sister!

"But Dad, Tigg started it!" protested Stripe. "She pulled my tail."

"I did not!" screeched Tigg. "And anyway, Stripe blew bubbles in my ear."

"Enough, you two," groaned Dad. He glanced at Cammie. "Are you all right?" he said gently. "You haven't eaten very much."

Cammie stared down at her bowl of plankton stew. Usually it was her favourite meal in the world, but she just didn't feel very hungry. "I'm okay," she said.

From across the table, Cammie's mother gave her an understanding smile. Cammie was dying to ask her whether the guards had put the sign up yet, but she knew better than to talk about the ghost net in front of Stripe and Tigg. It would really scare them.

"OW!" shrieked Tigg. "Stripe just pulled my tail, really hard!"

"Well, you pulled mine!" retorted Stripe.

Dad got up, looking thunderous. "All right, that's enough. Time for bed, you two."

"But that's not fair!" protested Stripe.

"Why should *I* have to leave the table?" wailed Tigg. "All I did was—"

"Both of you! Now!" ordered Dad.

Still arguing, Tigg and Stripe flounced away from the table, with Dad following along behind. Suddenly, it was much quieter with them gone!

"Mum—" started Cammie.

Her mother leaned across and patted her fin. "The other guards and I put a sign up like you suggested, warning creatures about the ghost net," she said. "Don't worry. It shouldn't hurt anyone now."

"Are you sure?" asked Cammie anxiously.

"As sure as I can be," said her mother. "The sign's a nice big one, so that everyone's sure to

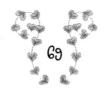

see it. And I'll try to keep an eye on the ghost net, in case it starts to drift."

Cammie let out a breath. That was good to hear…but she still couldn't help worrying. She knew that her mother had her guard duties to attend to. She and the other guards couldn't spend all their time watching the net.

"Come on, let's start clearing the table," said her mother. She smiled. "I think your dad's going to have his fins full for a while!"

Still deep in thought, Cammie began to stack the coral bowls. She wished so much that they could try to move the ghost net somewhere safe, where it wouldn't hurt the Reef or its creatures!

But the Queen had forbidden it.

*

"There!" said Jess, swimming back a bit and gazing at the coral. "It's looking a lot better, isn't it?"

"It really is," said Cammie. She had decided to help Jess with her project, since she still couldn't think of anything else to do. For several days now, the two friends had got together after school to clean the smudged piece of coral. It was looking much healthier now.

"Anyway, we'd better stop. It's time for our Pearlies meeting soon," said Jess, putting her sponge away in the shell bucket.

Cammie did the same with hers. "I guess we'll all be talking about our projects today, and how we're coming along with them," she said. Somehow, she just couldn't feel as excited about trying for her sixth pearl as she once had. Knowing that the ghost net was still out there cast a shadow over everything.

Jess giggled suddenly. "You know, I feel sort of sorry for those children Corinetta's reading to!" She tossed her head, imitating the golden seahorse. "Now, listen up, children! You are all *so* lucky to have wonderful *me* reading to you — I have a very tall crown, you know!"

Cammie managed a smile. Jess gave her a sympathetic look. "Oh, Cammie! What's wrong? Are you still worried about the ghost net?"

Cammie nodded glumly. "Sorry. I can't help it."

"I know…it's awful," agreed Jess. Then she brightened. "But who knows, maybe the tide's carried it away from Rainbow Reef by now. It could be gone for good!"

Cammie's heart quickened. *Could* the tide have carried the ghost net away? It had been several days, after all. It would be so wonderful if the net was really gone from Rainbow Reef!

Suddenly an idea came to Cammie. She glanced furtively around them. The only

creature in sight
was a stingray,
gliding past far
overhead. Just in
case, Cammie lowered her
voice anyway. "Jess," she whispered. "Let's go
and check!"

Her best friend stared at her. "What? But
we can't! We're supposed to keep away from
the ghost net."

"We won't get close to it," insisted Cammie.
"Just near enough to see whether it's still there
or not."

"But…we'll be late for Pearlies," said Jess
reluctantly.

"Not if we hurry." Grabbing Jess's bucket
from her, Cammie quickly put their supplies

away in Jess's family's coral shed. "Come on, we have time! It's not that far."

"Oh, Cammie..." Jess looked torn.

"Please?" Cammie urged. "Jess, I — I really have to know."

Finally Jess let out a breath. "Oh, all right," she said. "But Cammie, we're going to swim as fast as we can, take *one* quick peek, and then come straight back again! Right?"

"Right!" agreed Cammie with a grin. All at once she felt better than she had in days!

The two seahorses took off, jetting through the warm water. Somehow, it turned into a race, with Cammie in the lead. "Catch up, sea slug!" she called over her shoulder.

She zoomed around a cluster of rocks, giggling as Jess shouted, "I'll get you for that!"

Then Cammie slowed down, frowning. Wasn't the ghost net near here? Surely she should have spotted the *Danger* sign by now.

"Ha, I win!" cried Jess, darting past her.

Cammie grabbed her fin. "Jess, wait! There's something strange going on. I'm sure the ghost net's near here, but there's no sign."

Jess looked worried. "Well...are you certain this is the right place?"

"Yes, I'm positive! It was right—" Cammie broke off suddenly as a shout drifted towards them through the water. She and Jess stared at each other in horror.

"Did — did you hear that?" gasped Jess.

Cammie nodded, feeling almost sick with fear. Someone had been calling for help...and it had come from the direction of the ghost net.

She took a deep breath. "Come on!" she said. "We've got to go and help them!"

Chapter Six

"Help!" called the voice. "Please, help me!"

As Cammie and Jess drew closer, Cammie went cold. The ghost net had come partly undone from the coral, so that it was waving about in the water. And trapped in it was a young sea turtle!

Cammie and Jess hurried over to him.

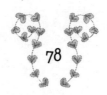

Though about their age, the sea turtle was much larger than they were, and his shell and flippers were badly tangled in the net. "Oh, thank goodness," he panted when he saw them. "I've been struggling for hours!"

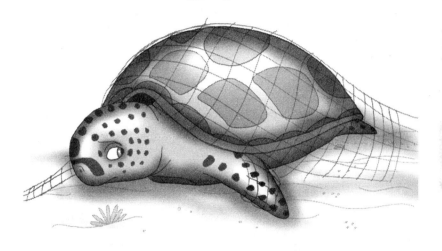

"But — wasn't there a sign?" gasped Jess.

The turtle shook his head wearily. "No, nothing. I was just swimming along, and then suddenly I was caught."

Cammie stared at him in dismay. The poor turtle seemed weak from his struggle — they had to help him, and fast! Grabbing hold of the net with her tail, Cammie started to tug.

"Jess, help me!" she cried. The two seahorses pulled and yanked, but nothing happened. The net stayed tightly wrapped about the turtle.

Cammie felt close to tears. What were they going to do? They couldn't just leave the turtle to his fate!

All at once an idea came to her. Archie! The crab didn't live far from here, and with his claws he could easily chop through the net. "I'll be right back!" she burst out.

Before Jess could respond, Cammie had darted away. Racing around pieces of coral and rocks, she soon arrived back at the funny little crab's house. It was just as tidy as she remembered, without even a grain of sand out of place.

Archie came bustling out of the cave when he heard her. "Oh, it's you," he said, clicking his claws. "Have you decided to come back and help me keep my cave clean?"

"Archie, I need your help!" cried Cammie, darting over to him. She explained what the problem was. "With your claws, you could easily cut through the net—" she started.

She broke off. Archie's eyes were bulging in alarm. He ducked back into his shell. "Sorry," he said, his voice muffled. "I've heard how dangerous ghost nets are! I don't think I can help you."

"But you have to!" protested Cammie. "The turtle won't be able to get free otherwise."

"Yes, pity," said Archie from deep inside his shell. Only his eyes were visible as he began to creep away back towards his cave. "But — but who would keep my cave tidy if anything happened to me? It's quite impossible, you see!"

Cammie started to argue again, and then gave up in despair. Archie wasn't going to help, that was clear! What was she going to do now?

Sadly, she started to turn away…and then something at the side of Archie's cave caught her gaze. Swimming forward, her eyes widened. It was a large sign written on a piece of driftwood. *DANGER, GHOST NET! KEEP AWAY!* it said.

"Archie! What's this sign doing here?" burst out Cammie.

The crab peeked out of his shell. "Oh — it was cluttering up the Reef, not far from here," he said. "I can't abide clutter! So I tidied it away."

"You *what*?" shrieked Cammie. "Didn't you read it?"

The crab's cheeks went bright red. "Er…I
can't actually…I mean, some of the words were
hard to make out…" He trailed off.

Suddenly Cammie understood. "Oh, Archie!
You can't read, can you?"

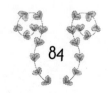

He winced. "No, not really," he admitted. "Did — did the sign say something important?"

"Yes, it was warning everyone about the ghost net!" cried Cammie. "The turtle wouldn't have got trapped in the first place, if you had left it there — you *must* help!"

Slowly, the crab came out of his shell. "You mean it's my fault?" he said in amazement.

"Yes!" said Cammie.

The crab opened and closed his mouth. He seemed lost for words. "Well, I suppose I'd better help, then," he grumbled finally. "I didn't mean to hurt anyone. I just wanted things to be neat and tidy, that's all."

"Come on, we have to hurry!" said Cammie urgently. She knew the turtle must be growing weaker by the minute.

With Archie scuttling along on the ocean floor below, Cammie rushed back to the ghost net. Jess was waiting beside the turtle, looking anxious. "There you are!" she burst out. Then she caught sight of Archie. "Who's that?"

"Someone who can help, I hope!" said Cammie.

Archie had reached the net and was shaking his head. "Oh, this won't do at all," he clucked. "I've never *seen* anything so untidy! It's got to go!" Pulling himself up the net by his claws, Archie reached the turtle. "But let's rescue *you* first, shall we?"

Cammie held her breath as he sawed at the net with his claws. Long moments passed with nothing happening. Cammie and Jess exchanged a worried look. Would Archie be

able to cut through the net after all? He was so
little compared to it!

But the hermit crab set his jaw and worked
harder. Finally, there was a *snip! snip!* and the
net around the turtle fell free. He swam dazedly
out from the net. "Thank you!" he gasped in
relief. "I thought I would never be free again!"

"And now let's see about getting rid of this
eyesore," said the crab. He scuttled across the

net. Cammie noticed sadly that a lot more of the coral had been broken since she'd last seen the ghost net.

"Ah-ha!" exclaimed Archie, finding the spot where the net was snagged on the coral. He started sawing with his claws, as hard as he could. "If I cut it here, we'll get rid of it!"

"Archie, wait!" said Cammie in alarm. "We can't just let it drift. It'll trap even *more* creatures that way—"

Snip! Snip!

It was too late. Even as she spoke, the net came free. Silently, it started to float off through the water.

Chapter Seven

"No!" screeched Cammie. She raced after the ghost net, grabbing it with her tail. But it was too heavy for her, and started to drag her with it. "Eek!" she screamed.

"Here, let me help!" cried the turtle. "I don't want anyone else to get tangled up the way I was." He grabbed a corner of the net with his

89

mouth. He was much bigger and stronger than Cammie. To her relief, she felt the net stop.

"We have to do something!" she said worriedly. "Or else it's just going to keep causing harm."

Jess nodded. "I'll go and get help!" She darted off through the water, leaving a trail of bubbles behind her.

"Well, that's a job well done," said Archie cheerfully, clambering down from the coral. "I'm glad that's over with! Now, I'd better get back to my cave. It might have got untidy again since I left."

"But — it's not over with at all!" cried Cammie, struggling to hold on to the net.

The hermit crab didn't seem to hear. He was already scuttling away, humming to himself. Soon he had disappeared in the distance. Cammie blew out a breath. At least Archie had got the sea turtle free — but *now* what were they meant to do?

Just then a corner of the net drifted onto

a lavender piece of coral, snapping it off. Cammie winced. She *couldn't* just let the ghost net float free in Rainbow Reef, no matter what the Queen said!

"Let's take the net to the Deep," she suggested to the turtle. "We've got to get it out of the Reef!"

"Good idea," said the turtle. "Come on!"

She and the turtle tugged at the net. But it was much harder to steer the ghost net than to just hold it in place. It seemed to want to go off in its own direction! Cammie gritted her teeth, pulling with all her might. The turtle, already tired from his struggle, wasn't doing much better. Slowly, the two of them started to drift away with the net.

"Cammie, hold on!" called Jess's voice.

Cammie turned her head as Jess came racing up — with all the rest of the Dancing Waves behind her!

"What are *you* doing here?" she gasped.

"We want to help," said Fizz firmly, grabbing hold of the ghost net with her tail. The others did the same. Cammie almost shouted with relief as the net slowed and stopped.

Bree nodded. "Jess told us what happened. We have to get rid of the ghost net. Even — even if the Queen's going to be angry with us. It's the right thing to do!"

Cammie's heart swelled as she gazed around her at her friends. Even Cora, usually so nervous, looked determined to help. And Corinetta, too! Cammie stared at her in amazement.

The golden seahorse looked embarrassed. "Yes, well," she muttered. "I live in Rainbow Reef too, don't I? I don't want to see the coral smashed up, or anyone hurt. Besides," she added, tossing her head, "you need *someone* who knows what they're doing."

"Yes, that's why we've got Cammie!" laughed Jess. "Where are we taking it, Cam?"

"To the Deep!" said Cammie eagerly.

The turtle had stayed silent through all of this, but now he nodded, his dark eyes gleaming. "Come on, everyone — pull!"

Cammie strained as hard as she could. With the turtle and her friends all helping, the net started moving slowly in the right direction. But it was hard work, and soon the seahorses were panting tiredly.

"What's going on?" called a voice. A large cod came swimming up, gaping at them. "Is that the ghost net? No one's supposed to touch it!"

Cammie gulped. "I know," she said. "But — but now it's come loose, and we can't just let it drift. So we're moving it away from Rainbow Reef."

Cod were big, but not very clever. As this one blinked, Cammie could practically see him thinking! "You're right!" he burst out. "I'm with you, little seahorse." Grabbing another corner of the net with his mouth, he started to tug as well. Cammie grinned. With his help, it was suddenly much easier!

"But — but the Queen!" gasped a parrotfish who was watching. He darted about the water anxiously, waving his fins.

"Bother the Queen!" boomed the cod.
"This ghost net's caused enough trouble. It's
time to take action — right, little seahorse?"
He looked at Cammie for support.

Cammie winced, wondering what the Rainbow Queen was going to say when she found out about this! "Right," she agreed weakly as the parrotfish scowled and sped away.

As they pulled the net towards the Deep, other creatures came swimming up to help, too.

Soon they'd been joined by an eel, a school of silvery fish, and three more turtles. The net was fairly gliding along now, moving rapidly.

"Whee!" cried Fizz, waving her fins. The seahorses weren't having to tug at all now, but were being pulled along rapidly with the net.

Cammie laughed despite herself, feeling the water rush past. It was even better than catching a ride on a pipefish!

Finally, they reached the edge of Rainbow Reef. Beyond lay the Deep. Cammie gazed down at its still, cold depths. Suddenly she wasn't sure what to do after all. What had she been thinking? They couldn't just release the net out into the Deep! It could hurt creatures there, too.

All at once Cammie realized that everyone was looking at her, waiting to hear what they should do now — even the cod and all the turtles! She bit her lip uncertainly. "Um..."

"Can I help?" said a friendly voice.

Cammie's eyes widened as a dolphin came swimming up from the Deep. He had smooth

grey skin and keen black eyes, and was much
larger than she was. He loomed in the water
above her.

The dolphin frowned when he saw the net.
"Urgh! What have you got one of *those* things
for?"

Cammie hastily explained. "And now I'm not sure what to do," she finished. "We have to make sure that the net doesn't hurt anyone."

"Hmm," said the dolphin. "What you really need is to give it to some humans, somehow. They're the only ones who'd be able to get rid of it safely."

The young turtle who'd been caught in the net looked unsure. "But it's because of humans that the net's here in the first place! I don't think we can count on *them* for help."

The dolphin shook his head. "No, there are nice humans too, as well as thoughtless ones. Some of them really care about the sea, and don't want anything to hurt it."

An idea started to come to Cammie. "Do you know any nice humans?" she asked slowly.

The dolphin smiled. "Yes, I do, actually. There are some who live not far from here. I often see them on the beach, cleaning up litter. They'd know what to do with this net—"

The dolphin stopped short as the same idea seemed to come to him. He and Cammie stared at each other. "Would you take it to them?" burst out Cammie. She shot up in the water as she fluttered her fins. "Oh, *please* say you will!"

The dolphin hesitated. "I'd be glad to, but... how will I move it without getting hurt myself?"

"I know — we'll roll it up into a ball!" said Cammie excitedly. "Come on, everyone!" Working together, she and the other creatures did so, and then tied the net together with strands of eelgrass.

"That'll do!" laughed the dolphin, nudging the ball with his long nose. "I'll be off now. The sooner we get rid of this, the better! Goodbye!" He sped off into the Deep, pushing the net ahead of him.

"Goodbye! Thank you!" called everyone. Cammie and her friends grinned at each other.

Hurrah! thought Cammie. She couldn't believe that the net was really gone!

Suddenly Cora bit her lip. "I wonder what's going to happen to us now?" she said in a shaky voice. "I mean…once the Queen hears what we've done."

Catching a glimpse of something out of the corner of her eye, Cammie's blood ran cold. "I – I think we're about to find out," she said faintly.

Chapter Eight

Cammie gulped. Swimming towards them in a stately procession was the Rainbow Queen herself, with a dozen other grand-looking seahorses gliding along behind her. The Queen looked very grim. Staring worriedly at them, Cammie blinked suddenly. Miss Swish was arriving, too, darting up from another direction. And *Mum*!

"Oh, we're in for it now," moaned Cora.

"It was worth it," said Fizz staunchly. "It was the right thing to do to get rid of that net, no matter what!"

Though Cammie agreed, she could hardly speak as the Queen drew up in front of her. She wore a different crown this time: gold, with gleaming pearls on it. "Is what I've heard from the parrotfish correct?" she demanded. "Have you really disobeyed my orders, and touched the ghost net?"

"Y-yes," stammered Cammie. "But — but you see—"

"Enough!" snapped the Queen, her eyes flashing. "It was a dangerous, foolhardy thing to do. And I won't have my orders ignored!"

Cammie hung her head wretchedly. Her

mother and Miss Swish arrived, jetting up through the water. Mum swam over to her and squeezed her tail. "Cammie, tell us what happened," she said.

"Yes, you have to let her talk!" burst out the young sea turtle. "She and her friends saved me. If it hadn't been for them, I'd still be trapped in that net!"

The Queen looked taken aback. "What's this? You were trapped in the net? But — there was a sign!"

"No, it — it got taken away," said Cammie. She stopped abruptly, not wanting to get Archie into trouble. Though he'd been very foolish to take away the sign when he didn't know what it said, he *had* helped the turtle once he realized what he'd done.

The Queen stared. "Taken away? But—"

"All I knew was that one moment I was

swimming along, and then the next I was

trapped!" exclaimed the

sea turtle, waving his

fins. "I was calling

for help for hours!"

Everyone went still

as he told the whole

story. He described how

Cammie and Jess had tried to help him, and

how Cammie had gone for the hermit crab.

"He was able to set me free!" said the turtle.

"And then, while her friend went to get more

help, this seahorse held the net with me." He

pointed at Cammie. "It's all because of her that

we got rid of the ghost net. She knew exactly

what to do!" He explained about Cammie's idea to take the net to the Deep, and how the dolphin had helped once they got there.

There was a long silence after he'd finished. The Queen stared at Cammie, her cape moving slowly in the current. Cammie swallowed hard, wondering what she was thinking.

Cammie's mother cleared her throat. "Your Majesty, I know that my daughter disobeyed you...but I'm proud of her," she said. "She may have saved this turtle's life — and the lives of other creatures, as well, by getting rid of the ghost net."

Cammie blinked as a warm glow spread through her, from her crown to the tip of her tail. Mum wasn't cross! She was actually *proud* of her.

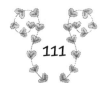

To Cammie's amazement, the Rainbow
Queen slowly started to nod. "Yes," she said. "I
agree that Cammie couldn't have left the turtle
to his fate. And…and perhaps I was wrong, to
order that no one should touch the net. I was
so afraid of anyone being hurt again, like my
son was. But Cammie, you've shown me what

strength there can be in numbers. If we all work together, we can succeed."

Cammie caught her breath in surprise. "Oh, Your Majesty, thank you!" she burst out. She and her friends grinned at each other in relief.

"No, thank *you*," said the Queen. "You've taught me a valuable lesson today." She smiled at the Dancing Waves. "I see that you're all Pearlies," she commented. "And that you each have five pearls. So you must be working on your Friend to the Reef pearl now, is that correct?"

Cammie nodded. "We're supposed to be trying for it soon."

The Queen laughed. "Well, I have a feeling it might happen sooner than you think!" She looked at Miss Swish. "Do you agree?"

"Yes, absolutely!" said Miss Swish. She beamed at the Dancing Waves. "And I couldn't be more pleased."

Cammie frowned in confusion. She wasn't completely sure what the Queen and Miss Swish were talking about. Unless...

She gasped as Queen Hortense took off her crown and handed it to Miss Swish.

Its beautiful pearls gleamed. "I'd like you to use my own pearls," said the Queen to Miss Swish. "As a special thank you from me!"

"You mean — we're about to become Seahorse Stars?" burst out Bree. Cammie's heart thudded as the Dancing Waves exchanged an excited look.

The Queen nodded. "Yes, you've earned your sixth pearl. You've all shown yourselves to be true friends to the Reef, by fighting against the ghost net and seeing that it was disposed of safely. Cammie, come forward. You shall be the first!"

In a daze, Cammie swam to Miss Swish. The Dancing Waves leader took one of the pearls from the Queen's shell crown and placed it onto Cammie's natural one. "Cammie, I am delighted to give you your sixth pearl, for being a friend to the reef," she said warmly. "You are now a Seahorse Star!"

The creatures around them all cheered, bobbing up and down in the water. Cammie could hardly speak. "Thank you!" she said to Miss Swish and the Queen. "Thank you so much!"

One by one, the other seahorses came forward, too, until all of them had six pearls shining on their crowns. Gazing upwards, Cammie thought that the Queen's pearl shone brightest of all.

"From now on, we'll all work together to get rid of ghost nets," said the Queen. "They won't hurt our Reef any longer." She smiled at Cammie. "And you know...I think, now that

you and your friends are Seahorse Stars, the
Reef is in very safe fins!"

Cammie's cheeks turned hot at the praise.
Before she could answer, the Queen had turned
and glided regally off through the water, her
attendants following after her.

"Well done, Cammie!" said Mum, squeezing her hard. "I'm so proud of you — so proud of all of you!" she said to the rest of the Dancing Waves.

"Yes, me too," said Miss Swish. "Now, would everyone like to come back to the Pearlie Pavilion with me? I think a celebration is in order, for our newest Seahorse Stars!" She beamed at them.

"We'll all come, too!" declared the cod. "We owe a lot to this little seahorse." He winked at Cammie, and she felt herself blush. She could never have imagined how this day would turn out!

Everyone headed back through the Reef, laughing and chatting. The Dancing Waves swam together in a group. "Hey, what about our projects?" said Bree suddenly. "We were all doing things to help the Reef."

"I think we should still do them," said Cora shyly. "I want to help the Reef more than ever, now that I'm a Seahorse Star."

"Yes, me too!" said Fizz. "I agree. Let's keep doing our projects anyway!"

Corinetta blinked. "What — you mean, even though we won't get a pearl for them?"

"Definitely!" cried Jess. She nudged Corinetta with her fin. "Come on, Corinetta. You know you love reading to those little seahorses!"

Corinetta considered it for a moment. "Well… I *suppose* I could keep doing it," she said grandly.

"After all, no one reads to them as well as *I* do. It would be a shame for me to stop."

"And then, once we've finished these projects, we can think of others to do!" cried Cammie. "We can *always* do things to help the Reef!"

Jess grinned at her. "Yes, because now we're..."

"SEAHORSE STARS!" cried all the girls joyfully, spinning in the water. They collapsed about laughing.

"Come on, girls!" called Miss Swish over her shoulder.

As the Dancing Waves hurried to catch up with Miss Swish and the others, Cammie gazed up at her sixth pearl. She shook her head slightly, smiling in wonder as it winked at her in

the sunlight. Though she could still hardly
believe it…she was really a Seahorse Star.
And now the adventures could begin!

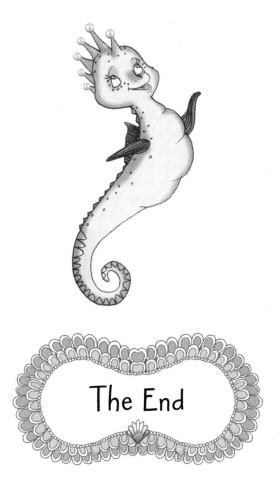

The End

Dive in with Cammie and her friends and
collect every splash-tastic tale in

Seahorse Stars!

The First Pearl ISBN 9781409520245

Cammie is thrilled to be a member of the Pearlies
— the waviest club in Rainbow Reef. Her first task
is to go camping. Will she keep her cool, or
is she in too deep?

First-Aid Friends ISBN 9781409520252

When Cammie's best friend shows a natural talent for
first-aid, Cammie gets competitive...and soon it's their
friendship that needs patching up!

The Lost Lagoon ISBN 9781409520269

Cammie is confused by compasses and lost when
it comes to maps, so earning her Wave Wanderer
pearl is proving tricky. When stuck-up Corinetta
offers to help, Cammie is grateful. But can
Corinetta be trusted?

Danger in the Deep ISBN 9781409520276

Cammie loves studying for her Sea Safety pearl
and learning about the dangers of the Deep. So when
her little sister disappears, it's up to Cammie
to rescue her...

Dancing Waves ISBN 9781409520306

All the seahorses must work together if they are
to earn their Tidal Team pearl...and they've chosen
Cammie as their team leader. Can she stop them
squabbling and help them come out on top?

The Rainbow Queen ISBN 9781409520313

To get her last Proficiency Pearl, Cammie must do
a good deed in Rainbow Reef...and then she will be a
Seahorse Star! But when Cammie begins her task, she
realizes the Reef is in danger, and she must ask
the Queen for help.

If you loved Seahorse Stars, dive into

Enchanted Shell ○ 9780746096154

Molly is transported to the Undersea Kingdom for the first
time, where she discovers she is the secret mermaid!

Seaside Adventure ○ 9780746096161

To help Ella recover her piece of the magical conch,
Molly must find a way to trap an angry killer whale.

Underwater Magic ○ 9780746096178

Can Molly find some pirate treasure to win back Delphi's
shell from a grumpy sea urchin?

Reef Rescue ○ 9780746096192

Molly must help Coral find her shell to restore the ocean
reefs, but a swarm of jellyfish stands in their way...

Deep Trouble ○ 9780746096185

Pearl's conch piece is trapped in an undersea volcano and
guarded by sea snakes. How can she and Molly release it?

Return of the Dark Queen ○ 9780746096208

Molly must save Shivana from an Arctic prison before the
Shell-Keeper mermaids can finally face the Dark Queen and
complete the magical conch.

by Sue Mongredien

Seahorse SOS ○ 9781409506324

There's more trouble in the Undersea Kingdom and Molly
joins in the search for the missing seahorses.

Dolphin Danger ○ 9781409506331

Molly and Aisha can hear faint calls for help but the
dolphins are nowhere to be seen. Where can they be?

Penguin Peril ○ 9781409506348

Could the Dark Queen be behind the mysterious
disappearance of the penguins from the icy seas?

Turtle Trouble ○ 9781409506355

There are some scary monsters lurking in the coral reef and
they're guarding the turtles Molly has come to set free!

Whale Rescue ○ 9781409506393

Molly must not only save the trapped whales but also her
mermaid friend, Leila.

The Dark Queen's Revenge ○ 9781409506409

The Dark Queen is back and she wants to rule the Undersea
Kingdom with her bad magic. Can Molly put
an end to her vile plans?

For more wonderfully wavy reads
check out
www.fiction.usborne.com